The Red Signal

D1523465

by
Agatha Christie

Grand Magazine, June 1924

The Red Signal

'No, but how too thrilling,' said pretty Mrs Eversleigh, opening her lovely, but slightly vacant eyes very wide. 'They always say women have a sixth sense; do you think it's true, Sir Alington?'

The famous alienist smiled sardonically. He had an unbounded contempt for the foolish pretty type, such as his fellow guest. Alington West was the supreme authority on mental disease, and he was fully alive to his own position and importance. A slightly pompous man of full figure.

'A great deal of nonsense is talked, I know that, Mrs Eversleigh. What does the term mean—a sixth sense?'

'You scientific men are always so severe. And it really is extraordinary the way one seems to positively know things sometimes—just know them, feel them, I mean—quite uncanny—it really is. Claire knows what I mean, don't you, Claire?'

She appealed to her hostess with a slight pout, and a tilted shoulder.

Claire Trent did not reply at once. It was a small dinner party, she and her husband, Violet Eversleigh, Sir Alington West, and his nephew, Dermot West, who was an old friend of Jack Trent's. Jack Trent himself, a somewhat heavy florid man, with a good-humoured smile, and a pleasant lazy laugh, took up the thread.

'Bunkum, Violet! Your best friend is killed in a railway accident. Straight away you remember that you dreamt of a black cat last Tuesday—marvellous, you felt all along that something was going to happen!'

'Oh, no, Jack, you're mixing up premonitions with intuition now. Come, now, Sir Alington, you must admit that premonitions are real?'

'To a certain extent, perhaps,' admitted the physician cautiously. 'But coincidence accounts for a good deal, and then there is the invariable tendency to make the most of a story afterwards—you've always got to take that into account.'

'I don't think there is any such thing as premonition,' said Claire Trent, rather abruptly. 'Or intuition, or a sixth sense, or any of the things we talk about so glibly. We go through life like a train rushing through the darkness to an unknown destination.'

'That's hardly a good simile, Mrs Trent,' said Dermot West, lifting his head for the first time and taking part in the discussion. There was a curious glitter in the clear grey eyes that shone out rather oddly from the deeply tanned face. 'You've forgotten the signals, you see.'

'The signals?'

'Yes, green if it's all right, and red—for danger!'

'Red—for danger—how thrilling!' breathed Violet Eversleigh.

Dermot turned from her rather impatiently.

'That's just a way of describing it, of course. Danger ahead! The red signal! Look out!'

Trent stared at him curiously.

'You speak as though it were an actual experience, Dermot, old boy.'

'So it is—has been, I mean.'

'Give us the yarn.'

'I can give you one instance. Out in Mesopotamia—just after the Armistice, I came into my tent one evening with the feeling strong upon me. Danger! Look out! Hadn't the ghost of a notion what it was all about. I made a round of the camp, fussed unnecessarily, took all precautions against an attack by hostile Arabs. Then I went back to my tent. As soon as I got inside, the feeling popped up again stronger than ever. Danger! In the end, I took a blanket outside, rolled myself up in it and slept there.'

'Well?'

'The next morning, when I went inside the tent, first thing I saw was a great knife arrangement—about half a yard long—struck down through my bunk, just where I would have lain. I soon found out about it—one of the Arab servants. His son had been shot as a spy. What have you got to say to that, Uncle Alington, as an example of what I call the red signal?'

The specialist smiled non-committally.

'A very interesting story, my dear Dermot.'

'But not one that you would accept unreservedly?'

'Yes, yes, I have no doubt that you had the premonition of danger, just as you state. But it is the origin of the premonition I dispute. According to you, it came from without, impressed by some outside source upon your mentality. But nowadays we find that nearly everything comes from within—from our subconscious self.'

'Good old subconscious,' cried Jack Trent. 'It's the jack-of-all-trades nowadays.'

Sir Alington continued without heeding the interruption.

'I suggest that by some glance or look this Arab had betrayed himself. Your conscious self did not notice or remember, but with your subconscious self it was otherwise. The subconscious never forgets. We believe, too, that it can reason and deduce quite independently of the higher or conscious will. Your subconscious self, then, believed that an attempt might be made to assassinate you, and succeeded in forcing its fear upon your conscious realization.'

'That sounds very convincing, I admit,' said Dermot, smiling.

'But not nearly so exciting,' pouted Mrs Eversleigh.

'It is also possible that you may have been subconsciously aware of the hate felt by the man towards you. What in old days used to be called telepathy certainly exists, though the conditions governing it are very little understood.'

'Have there been any other instances?' asked Claire of Dermot.

'Oh! yes, but nothing very pictorial—and I suppose they could all be explained under the heading of coincidence. I refused an invitation to a country house once, for no other reason than the hoisting of the "red signal". The place was burnt out during the week. By the way, Uncle Alington, where does the subconscious come in there?'

'I'm afraid it doesn't,' said Alington, smiling.

'But you've got an equally good explanation. Come, now. No need to be tactful with near relatives.'

'Well, then, nephew, I venture to suggest that you refused the invitation for the ordinary reason that you didn't much want to go, and that after the fire, you suggested to yourself that you had had a warning of danger, which explanation you now believe implicitly.'

'It's hopeless,' laughed Dermot. 'It's heads you win, tails I lose.'

'Never mind, Mr West,' cried Violet Eversleigh. 'I believe in your Red Signal implicitly. Is the time in Mesopotamia the last time you had it?'

'Yes—until—'

'I beg your pardon?'

'Nothing.'

Dermot sat silent. The words which had nearly left his lips were: 'Yes, until tonight.' They had come quite unbidden to his lips, voicing a thought which had as yet not been consciously realized, but he was aware at once that they were true. The Red Signal was looming up out of the darkness. Danger! Danger close at hand!

But why? What conceivable danger could there be here? Here in the house of his friends? At least—well, yes, there was that kind of danger. He looked at Claire Trent—her whiteness, her slenderness, the exquisite droop of her golden head. But that danger had been there for some time—it was never likely to get acute. For Jack Trent was his best friend, and more than his best friend, the man who had saved his life in Flanders and had been recommended for the VC for doing so. A good fellow, Jack, one of the best. Damned bad luck that he should have fallen in love with Jack's wife. He'd get over it some day, he supposed. A thing couldn't go on hurting like this for ever. One could starve it out—that was it, starve it out. It was not as though she would ever guess—and if she did guess, there was no danger of her caring. A statue, a beautiful statue, a thing of gold and ivory and pale pink coral . . . a toy for a king, not a real woman . . .

Claire . . . the very thought of her name, uttered silently, hurt him . . . He must get over it. He'd cared for women before . . . 'But not like this!' said something. 'Not like this.' Well, there it was. No danger there—heartache, yes, but not danger. Not the danger of the Red Signal. That was for something else.

He looked round the table and it struck him for the first time that it was rather an unusual little gathering. His uncle, for instance, seldom dined out in this small, informal way. It was not as though the Trents were old friends; until this evening Dermot had not been aware that he knew them at all.

To be sure, there was an excuse. A rather notorious medium was coming after dinner to give a séance. Sir Alington professed to be mildly interested in spiritualism. Yes, that was an excuse, certainly.

The word forced itself on his notice. An excuse. Was the séance just an excuse to make the specialist's presence at dinner natural? If so, what was the real object of his being here? A host of details came rushing into Dermot's mind, trifles unnoticed at the time, or, as his uncle would have said, unnoticed by the conscious mind.

The great physician had looked oddly, very oddly, at Claire more than once. He seemed to be watching her. She was uneasy under his scrutiny. She made little twitching motions with her hands. She was nervous, horribly nervous, and was it, could it be, frightened? Why was she frightened?

With a jerk, he came back to the conversation round the table. Mrs Eversleigh had got the great man talking upon his own subject.

'My dear lady,' he was saying, 'what is madness? I can assure you that the more we study the subject, the more difficult we find it to pronounce. We all practise a certain amount of self-deception, and when we carry it so far as to believe we are the Czar of Russia, we are shut up or restrained. But there is a long road before we reach that point. At what particular spot on it shall we erect a post and say, "On this side sanity, on the other madness?" It can't be done, you know. And I will tell you this, if the man suffering from a delusion happened to hold his tongue about it, in all probability we should never be able to distinguish him from a normal individual. The extraordinary sanity of the insane is a most interesting subject.'

Sir Alington sipped his wine with appreciation, and beamed upon the company.

'I've always heard they are very cunning,' remarked Mrs Eversleigh. 'Loonies, I mean.'

'Remarkably so. And suppression of one's particular delusion has a disastrous effect very often. All suppressions are dangerous, as psychoanalysis has taught us. The man who has a harmless eccentricity, and can indulge it as such, seldom goes over the border line. But the man'—he paused—'or woman who is to all appearance perfectly normal may be in reality a poignant source of danger to the community.'

His gaze travelled gently down the table to Claire, and then back again. He sipped his wine once more.

A horrible fear shook Dermot. Was that what he meant? Was that what he was driving at? Impossible, but—

'And all from suppressing oneself,' sighed Mrs Eversleigh. 'I quite see that one should be very careful always to—to express one's personality. The dangers of the other are frightful.'

'My dear Mrs Everslcigh,' expostulated the physician. 'You have quite misunderstood me. The cause of the mischief is in the physical matter of the brain—sometimes arising from some outward agency such as a blow; sometimes, alas, congenital.'

'Heredity is so sad,' sighed the lady vaguely. 'Consumption and all that.'

'Tuberculosis is not hereditary,' said Sir Alington drily.

'Isn't it? I always thought it was. But madness is! How dreadful. What else?'

'Gout,' said Sir Alington smiling. 'And colour blindness—the latter is rather interesting. It is transmitted direct to males, but is latent in females. So, while there are many colour-blind men, for a woman to be colour-blind, it must have been latent in her mother as well as present in her father—rather an unusual state of things to occur. That is what is called sex-limited heredity.'

'How interesting. But madness is not like that, is it?'

'Madness can be handed down to men or women equally,' said the physician gravely.

Claire rose suddenly, pushing back her chair so abruptly that it overturned and fell to the ground. She was very pale and the nervous motions of her fingers were very apparent.

'You—you will not be long, will you?' she begged. 'Mrs Thompson will be here in a few minutes now.'

'One glass of port, and I will be with you, for one,' declared Sir Alington. 'To see this wonderful Mrs Thompson's performance is what I have come for, is it not? Ha, ha! Not that I needed any inducement.' He bowed.

Claire gave a faint smile of acknowledgment and passed out of the room, her hand on Mrs Eversleigh's shoulder.

'Afraid I've been talking shop,' remarked the physician as he resumed his seat. 'Forgive me, my dear fellow.'

'Not at all,' said Trent perfunctorily.

He looked strained and worried. For the first time Dermot felt an outsider in the company of his friend. Between these two was a secret that even an old friend might not share. And yet the whole thing was fantastic and incredible. What had he to go upon? Nothing but a couple of glances and a woman's nervousness.

They lingered over their wine but a very short time, and arrived up in the drawing-room just as Mrs Thompson was announced.

The medium was a plump middle-aged woman, atrociously dressed in magenta velvet, with a loud rather common voice.

'Hope I'm not late, Mrs Trent,' she said cheerily. 'You did say nine o'clock, didn't you?'

'You are quite punctual, Mrs Thompson,' said Claire in her sweet, slightly husky voice. 'This is our little circle.'

No further introductions were made, as was evidently the custom. The medium swept them all with a shrewd, penetrating eye.

11

'I hope we shall get some good results,' she remarked briskly. 'I can't tell you how I hate it when I go out and I can't give satisfaction, so to speak. It just makes me mad. But I think Shiromako (my Japanese control, you know) will be able to get through all right tonight. I'm feeling ever so fit, and I refused the welsh rabbit, fond of toasted cheese though I am.'

Dermot listened, half amused, half disgusted. How prosaic the whole thing was! And yet, was he not judging foolishly? Everything, after all, was natural—the powers claimed by mediums were natural powers, as yet imperfectly understood. A great surgeon might be wary of indigestion on the eve of a delicate operation. Why not Mrs Thompson?

Chairs were arranged in a circle, lights so that they could conveniently be raised or lowered. Dermot noticed that there was no question of tests, or of Sir Alington satisfying himself as to the conditions of the séance. No, this business of Mrs Thompson was only a blind. Sir Alington was here for quite another purpose. Claire's mother, Dermot remembered, had died abroad. There had been some mystery about her . . . Hereditary . . .

With a jerk he forced his mind back to the surroundings of the moment.

Everyone took their places, and the lights were turned out, all but a small red-shaded one on a far table.

For a while nothing was heard but the low even breathing of the medium. Gradually it grew more and more stertorous. Then, with a suddenness that made Dermot jump, a loud rap came from the far end of the room. It was repeated from the other side. Then a perfect crescendo of raps was heard. They died away, and a sudden high peal of mocking laughter rang through the room. Then silence, broken by a voice utterly unlike that of Mrs Thompson, a high-pitched quaintly inflected voice.

'I am here, gentlemen,' it said. 'Yess, I am here. You wish to ask me things?'

'Who are you? Shiromako?'

'Yess. I Shiromako. I pass over long time ago. I work. I very happy.'

Further details of Shiromako's life followed. It was all very flat and uninteresting, and Dermot had heard it often before. Everyone was happy, very happy. Messages were given from vaguely described relatives, the description being so loosely worded as to fit almost any contingency. An elderly lady, the mother of someone present, held the floor for some time, imparting copy book maxims with an air of refreshing novelty hardly borne out by her subject matter.

'Someone else want to get through now,' announced Shiromako. 'Got a very important message for one of the gentlemen.'

There was a pause, and then a new voice spoke, prefacing its remark with an evil demoniacal chuckle.

'Ha, ha! Ha, ha, ha! Better not go home. Better not go home. Take my advice.'

'Who are you speaking to?' asked Trent.

'One of you three. I shouldn't go home if I were him. Danger! Blood! Not very much blood—quite enough. No, don't go home.' The voice grew fainter. 'Don't go home!'

It died away completely. Dermot felt his blood tingling. He was convinced that the warning was meant for him. Somehow or other, there was danger abroad tonight.

There was a sigh from the medium, and then a groan. She was coming round. The lights were turned on, and presently she sat upright, her eyes blinking a little.

'Go off well, my dear? I hope so.'

'Very good indeed, thank you, Mrs Thompson.'

'Shiromako, I suppose?'

'Yes, and others.'

Mrs Thompson yawned.

'I'm dead beat. Absolutely down and out. Does fairly take it out of you. Well, I'm glad it was a success. I was a bit afraid it mightn't be—afraid something disagreeable might happen. There's a queer feel about this room tonight.'

She glanced over each ample shoulder in turn, and then shrugged them uncomfortably.

'I don't like it,' she said. 'Any sudden deaths among any of you people lately?'

'What do you mean—among us?'

'Near relatives—dear friends? No? Well, if I wanted to be melodramatic, I'd say there was death in the air tonight. There, it's only my nonsense. Goodbye, Mrs Trent. I'm glad you've been satisfied.'

Mrs Thompson in her magenta velvet gown went out.

'I hope you've been interested, Sir Alington,' murmured Claire.

'A most interesting evening, my dear lady. Many thanks for the opportunity. Let me wish you good night. You are all going to a dance, are you not?'

'Won't you come with us?'

'No, no. I make it a rule to be in bed by half past eleven. Good night. Good night, Mrs Eversleigh. Ah! Dermot, I rather want to have a word with you. Can you come with me now? You can rejoin the others at the Grafton Galleries.'

'Certainly, uncle. I'll meet you there then, Trent.'

Very few words were exchanged between uncle and nephew during the short drive to Harley Street. Sir Alington made a semi-apology for dragging Dermot away, and assured him that he would only detain him a few minutes.

'Shall I keep the car for you, my boy?' he asked, as they alighted.

'Oh, don't bother, uncle. I'll pick up a taxi.'

'Very good. I don't like to keep Charlson up later than I can help. Good night, Charlson. Now where the devil did I put my key?'

The car glided away as Sir Alington stood on the steps vainly searching his pockets.

'Must have left it in my other coat,' he said at length. 'Ring the bell, will you? Johnson is still up, I dare say.'

The imperturbable Johnson did indeed open the door within sixty seconds.

'Mislaid my key, Johnson,' explained Sir Alington. 'Bring a couple of whiskies and sodas into the library, will you?'

'Very good, Sir Alington.'

The physician strode on into the library and turned on the lights. He motioned to Dermot to close the door behind him after entering.

'I won't keep you long, Dermot, but there's just something I want to say to you. Is it my fancy, or have you a certain— tendresse, shall we say, for Mrs Jack Trent?'

The blood rushed to Dermot's face.

'Jack Trent is my best friend.'

'Pardon me, but that is hardly answering my question. I dare say that you consider my views on divorce and such matters highly puritanical, but I must remind you that you are my only near relative and that you are my heir.'

'There is no question of a divorce,' said Dermot angrily.

'There certainly is not, for a reason which I understand perhaps better than you do. That particular reason I cannot give you now, but I do wish to warn you. Claire Trent is not for you.'

The young man faced his uncle's gaze steadily.

'I do understand—and permit me to say, perhaps better than you think. I know the reason for your presence at dinner tonight.'

'Eh?' The physician was clearly startled. 'How did you know that?'

'Call it a guess, sir. I am right, am I not, when I say that you were there in your—professional capacity.'

Sir Alington strode up and down.

'You are quite right, Dermot. I could not, of course, have told you so myself, though I am afraid it will soon be common property.'

Dermot's heart contracted.

'You mean that you have—made up your mind?'

'Yes, there is insanity in the family—on the mother's side. A sad case—a very sad case.'

'I can't believe it, sir.'

'I dare say not. To the layman there are few if any signs apparent.'

'And to the expert?'

'The evidence is conclusive. In such a case, the patient must be placed under restraint as soon as possible.'

'My God!' breathed Dermot. 'But you can't shut anyone up for nothing at all.'

'My dear Dermot! Cases are only placed under restraint when their being at large would result in danger to the community.'

'Danger?'

'Very grave danger. In all probability a peculiar form of homicidal mania. It was so in the mother's case.'

Dermot turned away with a groan, burying his face in his hands. Claire—white and golden Claire!

'In the circumstances,' continued the physician comfortably, 'I felt it incumbent on me to warn you.'

'Claire,' murmured Dermot. 'My poor Claire.'

'Yes, indeed, we must all pity her.'

Suddenly Dermot raised his head.

'I don't believe it.'

'What?'

'I say I don't believe it. Doctors make mistakes. Everyone knows that. And they're always keen on their own speciality.'

'My dear Dermot,' cried Sir Alington angrily.

'I tell you I don't believe it—and anyway, even if it is so, I don't care. I love Claire. If she will come with me, I shall take her away—far away—out of the reach of meddling physicians. I shall guard her, care for her, shelter her with my love.'

'You will do nothing of the sort. Are you mad?'

Dermot laughed scornfully.

'You would say so, I dare say.'

'Understand me, Dermot.' Sir Alington's face was red with suppressed passion. 'If you do this thing—this shameful thing —it is the end. I shall withdraw the allowance I am now making you, and I shall make a new will leaving all I possess to various hospitals.'

'Do as you please with your damned money,' said Dermot in a low voice. 'I shall have the woman I love.'

'A woman who—'

'Say a word against her, and, by God! I'll kill you!' cried Dermot.

A slight clink of glasses made them both swing round. Unheard by them in the heat of their argument, Johnson had entered with a tray of glasses. His face was the imperturbable one of the good servant, but Dermot wondered how much he had overheard.

'That'll do, Johnson,' said Sir Alington curtly. 'You can go to bed.'

'Thank you, sir. Good night, sir.'

Johnson withdrew.

The two men looked at each other. The momentary interruption had calmed the storm.

'Uncle,' said Dermot. 'I shouldn't have spoken to you as I did. I can quite see that from your point of view you are perfectly right. But I have loved Claire Trent for a long time. The fact that Jack Trent is my best friend has hitherto stood in the way of my ever speaking of love to Claire herself. But in these circumstances that fact no longer counts. The idea that any monetary conditions can deter me is absurd. I think we've both said all there is to be said. Good night.'

'Dermot—'

'It is really no good arguing further. Good night, Uncle Alington. I'm sorry, but there it is.'

He went out quickly, shutting the door behind him. The hall was in darkness. He passed through it, opened the front door and emerged into the street, banging the door behind him.

A taxi had just deposited a fare at a house farther along the street and Dermot hailed it, and drove to the Grafton Galleries.

In the door of the ballroom he stood for a minute bewildered, his head spinning. The raucous jazz music, the smiling women—it was as though he had stepped into another world.

Had he dreamt it all? Impossible that that grim conversation with his uncle should have really taken place. There was Claire floating past, like a lily in her white and silver gown that fitted sheathlike to her slenderness. She smiled at him, her face calm and serene. Surely it was all a dream.

The dance had stopped. Presently she was near him, smiling up into his face. As in a dream he asked her to dance. She was in his arms now, the raucous melodies had begun again.

He felt her flag a little.

'Tired? Do you want to stop?'

'If you don't mind. Can we go somewhere where we can talk? There is something I want to say to you.'

Not a dream. He came back to earth with a bump. Could he ever have thought her face calm and serene? It was haunted with anxiety, with dread. How much did she know?

He found a quiet corner, and they sat down side by side.

'Well,' he said, assuming a lightness he did not feel. 'You said you had something you wanted to say to me?'

'Yes.' Her eyes were cast down. She was playing nervously with the tassel of her gown. 'It's difficult—rather.'

'Tell me, Claire.'

'It's just this. I want you to—to go away for a time.'

He was astonished. Whatever he had expected, it was not this.

'You want me to go away? Why?'

'It's best to be honest, isn't it? I—I know that you are a—a gentleman and my friend. I want you to go away because I—I have let myself get fond of you.'

'Claire.'

Her words left him dumb—tongue-tied.

'Please do not think that I am conceited enough to fancy that you—that you would ever be likely to fall in love with me. It is only that—I am not very happy—and—oh! I would rather you went away.'

'Claire, don't you know that I have cared—cared damnably—ever since I met you?'

She lifted startled eyes to his face.

'You cared? You have cared a long time?'

'Since the beginning.'

'Oh!' she cried. 'Why didn't you tell me? Then? When I could have come to you! Why tell me now when it's too late. No, I'm mad—I don't know what I'm saying. I could never have come to you.'

'Claire, what did you mean when you said "now that it's too late?" Is it—is it because of my uncle? What he knows? What he thinks?'

She nodded dumbly, the tears running down her face.

'Listen, Claire, you're not to believe all that. You're not to think about it. Instead you will come away with me. We'll go to the South Seas, to islands like green jewels. You will be happy there, and I will look after you—keep you safe for always.'

His arms went round her. He drew her to him, felt her tremble at his touch. Then suddenly she wrenched herself free.

'Oh, no, please. Can't you see? I couldn't now. It would be ugly—ugly—ugly. All along I've wanted to be good—and now—it would be ugly as well.'

He hesitated, baffled by her words. She looked at him appealingly.

'Please,' she said. 'I want to be good . . .'

Without a word, Dermot got up and left her. For the moment he was touched and racked by her words beyond argument. He went for his hat and coat, running into Trent as he did so.

'Hallo, Dermot, you're off early.'

'Yes, I'm not in the mood for dancing tonight.'

'It's a rotten night,' said Trent gloomily. 'But you haven't got my worries.'

Dermot had a sudden panic that Trent might be going to confide in him. Not that—anything but that!

'Well, so long,' he said hurriedly. 'I'm off home.'

'Home, eh? What about the warning of the spirits?'

'I'll risk that. Good night, Jack.'

Dermot's flat was not far away. He walked there, feeling the need of the cool night air to calm his fevered brain.

He let himself in with his key and switched on the light in the bedroom.

And all at once, for the second time that night, the feeling that he had designated by the title of the Red Signal surged over him. So overpowering was it that for the moment it swept even Claire from his mind.

Danger! He was in danger. At this very moment, in this very room, he was in danger.

He tried in vain to ridicule himself free of the fear. Perhaps his efforts were secretly half-hearted. So far, the Red Signal had given him timely warning which had enabled him to avoid disaster. Smiling a little at his own superstition, he made a careful tour of the flat. It was possible that some malefactor had got in and was lying concealed there. But his search revealed nothing. His man Milson, was away, and the flat was absolutely empty.

He returned to his bedroom and undressed slowly, frowning to himself. The sense of danger was acute as ever. He went to a drawer to get out a handkerchief, and suddenly stood stock still. There was an unfamiliar lump in the middle of the drawer—something hard.

His quick nervous fingers tore aside the handkerchiefs and took out the object concealed beneath them. It was a revolver.

With the utmost astonishment Dermot examined it keenly. It was of a somewhat unfamiliar pattern, and one shot had been fired from it lately. Beyond that, he could make nothing of it. Someone had placed it in that drawer that very evening. It had not been there when he dressed for dinner—he was sure of that.

He was about to replace it in the drawer, when he was startled by a bell ringing. It rang again and again, sounding unusually loud in the quietness of the empty flat.

Who could it be coming to the front door at this hour? And only one answer came to the question—an answer instinctive and persistent.

'Danger—danger—danger . . .'

Led by some instinct for which he did not account, Dermot switched off his light, slipped on an overcoat that lay across a chair, and opened the hall door.

Two men stood outside. Beyond them Dermot caught sight of a blue uniform. A policeman!

'Mr West?' asked the foremost of the two men.

It seemed to Dermot that ages elapsed before he answered. In reality it was only a few seconds before he replied in a very fair imitation of his man's expressionless voice:

'Mr West hasn't come in yet. What do you want with him at this time of night?'

'Hasn't come in yet, eh? Very well, then, I think we'd better come in and wait for him.'

'No, you don't.'

'See here, my man, my name is Inspector Verall of Scotland Yard, and I've got a warrant for the arrest of your master. You can see it if you like.'

Dermot perused the proffered paper, or pretended to do so, asking in a dazed voice:

'What for? What's he done?'

'Murder. Sir Alington West of Harley Street.'

His brain in a whirl, Dermot fell back before his redoubtable visitors. He went into the sitting-room and switched on the light. The inspector followed him.

'Have a search round,' he directed the other man. Then he turned to Dermot.

'You stay here, my man. No slipping off to warn your master. What's your name, by the way?'

'Milson, sir.'

'What time do you expect your master in, Milson?'

'I don't know, sir, he was going to a dance, I believe. At the Grafton Galleries.'

'He left there just under an hour ago. Sure he's not been back here?'

'I don't think so, sir. I fancy I should have heard him come in.'

At this moment the second man came in from the adjoining room. In his hand he carried the revolver. He took it across to the inspector in some excitement. An expression of satisfaction flitted across the latter's face.

'That settles it,' he remarked. 'Must have slipped in and out without your hearing him. He's hooked it by now. I'd better be off. Cawley, you stay here, in case he should come back again, and you keep an eye on this fellow. He may know more about his master than he pretends.'

The inspector bustled off. Dermot endeavoured to get at the details of the affair from Cawley, who was quite ready to be talkative.

'Pretty clear case,' he vouchsafed. 'The murder was discovered almost immediately. Johnson, the manservant, had only just gone up to bed when he fancied he heard a shot, and came down again. Found Sir Alington dead, shot through the heart. He rang us up at once and we came along and heard his story.'

'Which made it a pretty clear case?' ventured Dermot.

'Absolutely. This young West came in with his uncle and they were quarrelling when Johnson brought in the drinks. The old boy was threatening to make a new will, and your master was talking about shooting him. Not five minutes later the shot was heard. Oh! yes, clear enough. Silly young fool.'

Clear enough indeed. Dermot's heart sank as he realized the overwhelming nature of the evidence against him. Danger indeed—horrible danger! And no way out save that of flight. He set his wits to work. Presently he suggested making a cup of tea. Cawley assented readily enough. He had already searched the flat and knew there was no back entrance.

Dermot was permitted to depart to the kitchen. Once there he put the kettle on, and chinked cups and saucers industriously. Then he stole swiftly to the window and lifted the sash. The flat was on the second floor, and outside the window was a small wire lift used by tradesmen which ran up and down on its steel cable.

Like a flash Dermot was outside the window and swinging himself down the wire rope. It cut into his hands, making them bleed, but he went on desperately.

A few minutes later he was emerging cautiously from the back of the block. Turning the corner, he cannoned into a figure standing by the sidewalk. To his utter amazement he recognized Jack Trent. Trent was fully alive to the perils of the situation.

'My God! Dermot! Quick, don't hang about here.'

Taking him by the arm, he led him down a by-street, then down another. A lonely taxi was sighted and hailed and they jumped in, Trent giving the man his own address.

'Safest place for the moment. There we can decide what to do next to put those fools off the track. I came round here hoping to be able to warn you before the police got here, but I was too late.'

'I didn't even know that you had heard of it. Jack, you don't believe—'

'Of course not, old fellow, not for one minute. I know you far too well. All the same, it's a nasty business for you. They came round asking questions—what time you got to the Grafton Galleries, when you left, etc. Dermot, who could have done the old boy in?'

'I can't imagine. Whoever did it put the revolver in my drawer, I suppose. Must have been watching us pretty closely.'

'That séance business was damned funny. "Don't go home." Meant for poor old West. He did go home, and got shot.'

'It applies to me to,' said Dermot. 'I went home and found a planted revolver and a police inspector.'

'Well, I hope it doesn't get me too,' said Trent. 'Here we are.'

He paid the taxi, opened the door with his latch-key, and guided Dermot up the dark stairs to his den, which was a small room on the first floor.

He threw open the door and Dermot walked in, whilst Trent switched on the light, and then came to join him.

'Pretty safe here for the time being,' he remarked. 'Now we can get our heads together and decide what is best to be done.'

'I've made a fool of myself,' said Dermot suddenly. 'I ought to have faced it out. I see more clearly now. The whole thing's a plot. What the devil are you laughing at?'

For Trent was leaning back in his chair, shaking with unrestrained mirth. There was something horrible in the sound—something horrible, too, about the man altogether. There was a curious light in his eyes.

'A damned clever plot,' he gasped out. 'Dermot, my boy, you're done for.'

He drew the telephone towards him.

'What are you going to do?' asked Dermot.

'Ring up Scotland Yard. Tell 'em their bird's here—safe under lock and key. Yes, I locked the door when I came in and the key's in my pocket. No good looking at that other door behind me. That leads into Claire's room, and she always locks it on her side. She's afraid of me, you know. Been afraid of me a long time. She always knows when I'm thinking about that knife—a long sharp knife. No, you don't —'

Dermot had been about to make a rush at him, but the other had suddenly produced an ugly-looking revolver.

'That's the second of them,' chuckled Trent. 'I put the first of them in your drawer—after shooting old West with it—What are you looking at over my head? That door? It's no use, even if Claire was to open it—and she might to you—I'd shoot you before you got there. Not in the heart—not to kill, just wing you, so that you couldn't get away. I'm a jolly good shot, you know. I saved your life once. More fool I. No, no, I want you hanged—yes, hanged. It isn't you I want the knife for. It's Claire—pretty Claire, so white and soft. Old West knew. That's what he was here for tonight, to see if I was mad or not. He wanted to shut me up—so that I shouldn't get Claire with the knife. I was very cunning. I took his latchkey and yours too. I slipped away from the dance as soon as I got there. I saw you come out from his house, and I went in. I shot him and came away at once. Then I went to your place and left the revolver. I was at the Grafton Galleries again almost as soon as you were, and I put the latch-key back in your coat pocket when I was saying good night to you. I don't mind telling you all this. There's no one else to hear, and when you're being hanged I'd like you to know I did it . . . There's not a loophole of escape. It makes me laugh . . . God, how it makes me laugh! What are you thinking of? What the devil are you looking at?'

'I'm thinking of some words you quoted just now. You'd have done better, Trent, not to come home.'

'What do you mean?'

'Look behind you!' Trent spun round. In the doorway of the communicating room stood Claire—and Inspector Verall . . .

Trent was quick. The revolver spoke just once—and found its mark. He fell forward across the table. The inspector sprang to his side, as Dermot stared at Claire in a dream. Thoughts flashed through his brain disjointedly. His uncle—their quarrel—the colossal misunderstanding—the divorce laws of England which would never free Claire from an insane husband—'we must all pity her'—the plot between her and Sir Alington which the cunning of Trent had seen through—her cry to him, 'Ugly—ugly—ugly!' Yes, but now—

The inspector straightened up again.

'Dead,' he said vexedly.

'Yes,' Dermot heard himself saying, 'he was always a good shot . . .'

Made in the USA
Middletown, DE
08 December 2024

66366375R20018